The Old Tree Stories

Hungry
Mr Fox

First published in Great Britain in 1989 by
Belitha Press Limited
31 Newington Green, London N16 9PU

Printed in Hong Kong for Imago Publishing

British Library Cataloguing in Publication Data
Firmin, Peter
  Hungry Mr. Fox.
  I. Title   II. Series
  823'.914[J]

ISBN 0-947553-03-7

PETER FIRMIN

The Old Tree Stories

Hungry Mr Fox

Belitha Press

Mr Fox was hiding at the bottom
of the Old Tree.
He said: "I'd like something tasty
for dinner."

There was a fence near the tree.
There was a gap in the fence.
Through the gap came
a plump little mouse.

Mr Fox jumped out.
He caught the mouse and said:
"I'll gobble you up for
my dinner, nibble, nibble!"

The mouse said:
"Oh, don't spoil your dinner
with a mouthful like me.
There's a much better
meal coming soon."
So he let the mouse go.

Mr Fox waited at the bottom
of the Old Tree.
He said: "I shall have something
tasty for my dinner."

Through the gap in the fence came a very fat rat.

Mr Fox jumped out.
He caught the rat by the tail.
He said: "I'll gobble you up
for my dinner, yum, yum!"

But the rat said:
"Never eat snacks between
meals. Besides, there's someone
much fatter back there."

So Mr Fox let the rat go.

Mr Fox waited at the bottom
of the Old Tree. He said:
"I *must* have something
tasty for my dinner."

Through the gap in the fence,
with a leap and a jump, came a hare,
and Mr Fox said: "Now here's
something tasty for dinner!"

Mr Fox grabbed her
and held her and said:
"I'll gobble you up for
my dinner, SNAP, SNAP!"

The hare said: "Don't you think
I'd unsettle your tum? There's
something much bigger back there."
So he let the hare go.

Mr Fox waited and what did he see?
A big brown whiskery nose.

He jumped out and grabbed it
and bit it and said:
"You're not a mouse, rat or hare
but whatever you are,
I'll gobble you up
for my dinner, CRUNCH, CRUNCH!"

A big angry bear jumped
out through the gap.
He said: "You greedy old fox.
You'd better not gobble
the mouse or the rat
or the hare . . .
and especially not ME!"

He tossed
Mr Fox
high up into
the tree . . .

and the mouse and the hare and
the rat and the bear went
into the field for their dinner,
MUNCH, MUNCH.